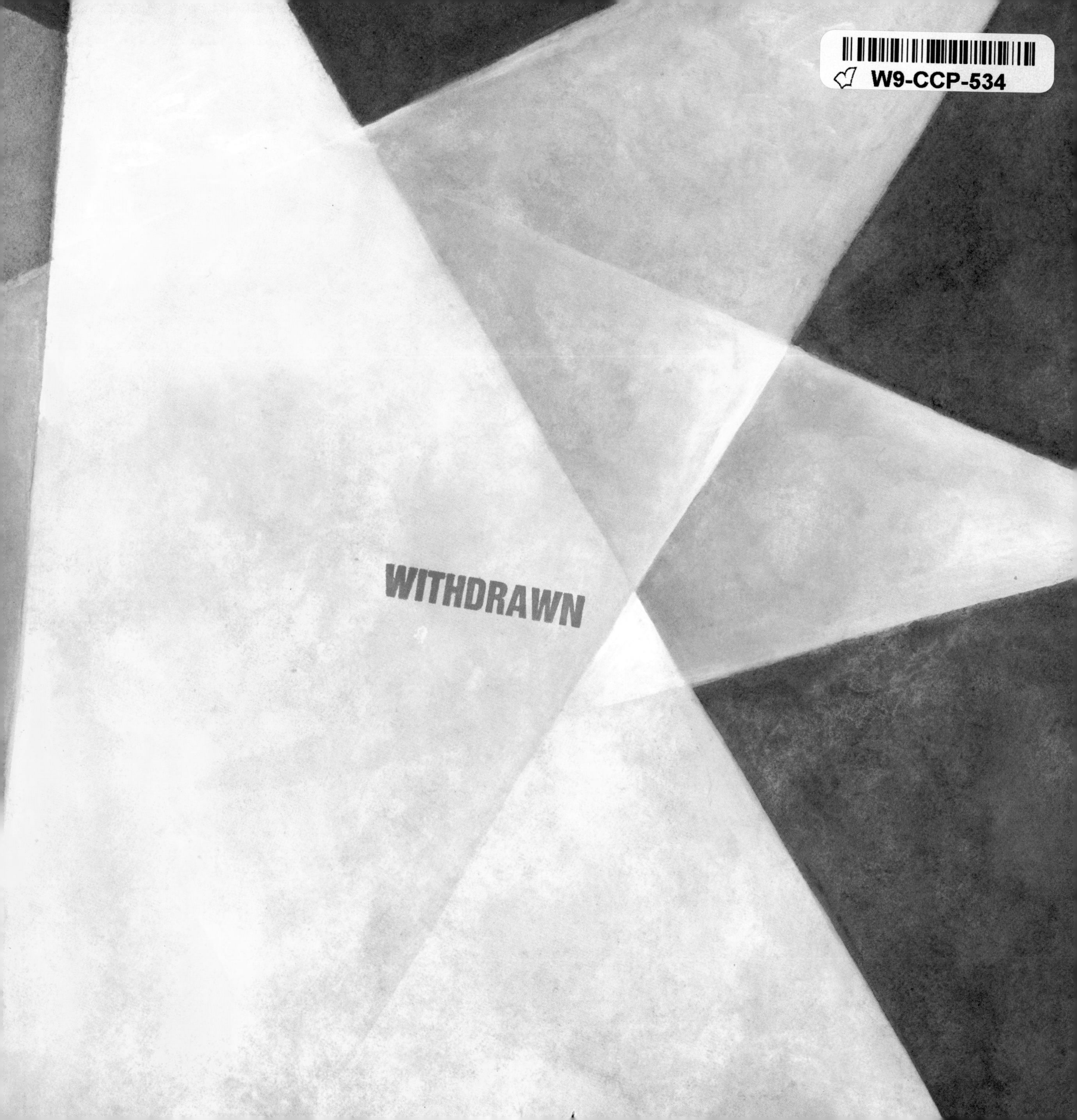

I'm Really Not Tired

Written by Lori Sunshine

Illustrated by Jeffrey Ebbeler

Flash
Light
PRESS

For Joshua and Sara – LS

For Cedric – JE

Copyright © 2008 by Flashlight Press
Text copyright © 2008 by Lori Sunshine
Illustrations copyright © 2008 by Jeffrey Ebbeler

All rights reserved, including the right of reproduction, in whole or in part, in any form.
Printed at Hemed Press, Israel.
First Edition – September 2008

Library of Congress Control Number: 2008925642

ISBN 978-0-9799746-1-8

Editor: Shari Dash Greenspan
Graphic Design: The Virtual Paintbrush
This book was typeset in Jot.
Illustrations were rendered in acrylic paint.

Distributed by Independent Publishers Group

Flashlight Press • 527 Empire Blvd. • Brooklyn, NY 11225
www.FlashlightPress.com

"I'm really not tired!"
called Samuel McKay
as he climbed into bed at the end of the day.
"I want to stay up. It's not even that late."
"It's bedtime," Dad said.
"It's a quarter to eight."

But Sam was quite certain the fun must begin
after teeth-brushing, face-washing, and tucking-in.
He was sure he was missing all *kinds* of great fun
that went on when his folks said the day was all done.

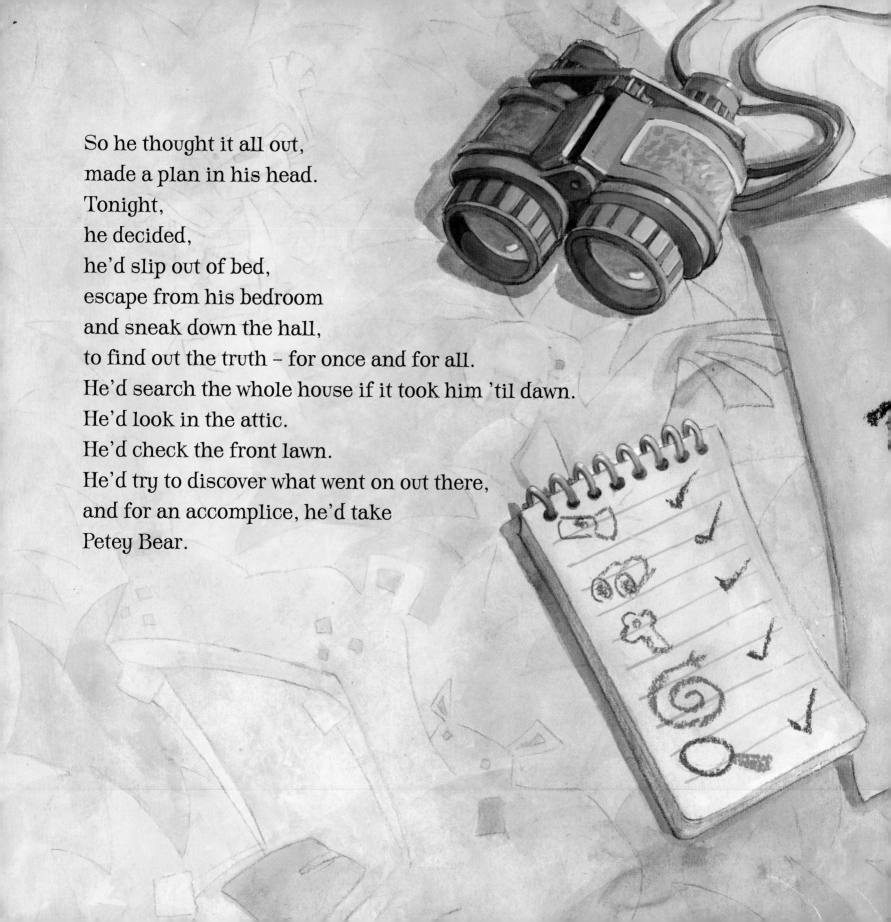

So he thought it all out,
made a plan in his head.
Tonight,
he decided,
he'd slip out of bed,
escape from his bedroom
and sneak down the hall,
to find out the truth – for once and for all.
He'd search the whole house if it took him 'til dawn.
He'd look in the attic.
He'd check the front lawn.
He'd try to discover what went on out there,
and for an accomplice, he'd take
Petey Bear.

Sam waited while Dad tucked him in
snug and tight,
and kissed him and wished him
sweet dreams for the night.
He waited while Dad
shut the light and the door.
Then Sam
      slid
        his
          tippy-toes
            back to the floor.

"Tonight's the night, Petey. Don't make any noise.
We'll find out if Mommy is playing with toys.
I bet Dad plays video games that go beep
while WE have to stay in our bedroom and *sleep*!
Or maybe they're eating pink ice cream and cake,"
Sam whispered to Petey.
"Good thing we're awake."

Across the thick carpet
they started to wriggle.
They got to the door
without one tiny giggle.
Sam pulled just a bit
so the door wouldn't squeak...

...and into the hallway they started to sneak.
"Could there be a *circus* camped out
in the kitchen
with lions and tigers?"
They stood still to listen.
"I think I hear clowns juggling
apples and fire.
I bet there's an acrobat on a high wire,
and horses
and elephants
AND chimpanzees,
and Dad swinging Mom on a
flying trapeze!"

"We miss all the fun, Pete.
It's really not fair,"
Sam said as they slid
on their seats
down a stair.
"Could our basement be filled with
a *thousand* toy trains?
Does our bathroom have *fish*
swimming up all the drains?"

Down the steps, one by one,
they continued to sneak.
They were doing just fine
'til the fifth step went

CREAK!

"Get back into bed,"
they heard Mom and Dad shout.

How Sam and Pete ran.
They had just been
found out!

They flew up the hall to their room, out of breath.

"Poor Petey," Sam whispered, "you look scared to death."

They jumped into bed, pulled the covers up high,
pretended to sleep – and then let out a sigh.
Sam's sheets were so smooth
and his soft pillow beckoned.
He thought about sleeping,
but just for a second.
He rubbed his eyes once,
and rubbed Petey's eyes too.

"Ooh! Maybe the guest room's
turned into a..."

"...ZOO!!
And monkeys are swinging
around on the drapes
and hippos and parrots
are all eating grapes!
Aw, Petey, we have to go
through with this plan.
We'll just tiptoe quieter.
I know we can."

SO...

...they pittered and pattered,

they tiptoed and crept,

then over the creaky stair carefully stepped.

"I bet there's a *rocket* in Dad's parking place with astronauts waiting to blast into space."

They scooched
two more steps
as they stifled a yawn.

"Oooh, maybe a T. rex is out on the lawn.
In just a few seconds, Pete, I'm *sure* we'll see,
the best fun goes on here *without* you and me!"

They silently slid
       to the very
             last
                 stair.
"We're finally here
at the den, Petey Bear."

And now was the moment.
Sam gripped Petey's paw.
He twisted his head
'round the corner
and saw...

...his mother and dad doing *nothing at all!*

"That's it?"
Sam complained, as they hid in the hall.
It wasn't at all how he'd pictured those scenes.
Dad worked on the crossword.
Mom read magazines.

Where were the monkeys,
            the ice cream,
                    the cake?

Was THIS all he missed when he wasn't awake?

So Sam McKay sighed and trudged back to his bed.
He pulled his soft blanket right up to his head.
"I guess we just missed it, Pete," Sam said with sorrow.
"We'll have to be quicker when we try tomorrow."
He hugged Petey Bear and repeated once more,
"I'm really not tired..."
then started to snore.

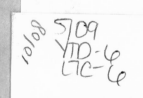